Roshni
Children's Books

UNESCO WORLD HERITAGE SITES OF INDIA SERIES

United Nations
Educational, Scientific and
Cultural Organization

Keoladeo Bird Sanctuary

The Kingdom of Birds

Author Erach Bharucha
Artist Maya Ramaswamy

MAPIN PUBLISHING

Sometimes, one small incident can change the direction of our lives.

In 1906 in Mumbai, a young boy was playing with his toy air gun. He took a playful shot at a sparrow and the bird thudded to the ground, dead! The boy was so upset about what he had done that he vowed to find out more about birds and do everything he could to help them thrive.

This boy was Salim Ali, the famous ornithologist.

He also helped to create the Keoladeo National Park—a bird sanctuary in Bharatpur— which is where our story begins!

Early one December morning, a group of young students from classes VII and VIII travelled from Agra to spend a day at the Keoladeo National Park to learn more about nature.

They enjoyed their experience so much that one of them, Dev, said, "I want to be an ornithologist too!"

What had he seen that made him say that? Let's find out!

The children got off the bus at the gate of the sanctuary and walked in. It was like stepping into a different world! Quiet and green, with soft earth on the paths. There was no screeching and honking of vehicles, only the hushed tinkle of bicycles and cycle-rickshaws, and the gentle patter of the drivers, who also acted as guides.

The children were met by Dr. Kranti Yardi, a zoologist, Rupa Ma'am, and Dr. Erach "Doc" Bharucha, a surgeon who also knew a lot about birds. A local guide showed them his telescope, which was pointed at a far-off tree. The children crowded around the telescope in curiosity and zoomed in on a group of pied mynas sitting on the tree.

"Be careful not to move the telescope, or it will shift away from the birds on which I have focused it," the guide said.

Doc had been interested in wildlife conservation for a long time and had been coming to the sanctuary for many years. What was so interesting about this sanctuary, wondered the children, that someone would visit so many times?

Pied Mynas

Flameback
Common
Kingfisher
Purple Heron

Slowly, as they looked around through the early morning mist, they began to realise the sanctuary was not actually quiet. There were dozens of birds, talking and twittering, or flying around playfully or looking for something to eat! Just like the children moved about in groups, the birds too tended to be in groups, constantly chirping or lifting off into the sky with a swish of their wings.

The birds were unpredictable too—one minute they would be sitting still on a branch but in the blink of an eye—*whoosh*!—they would fly away. The only way to observe them was to keep still and patient, but the children were so excited that it took them some time to quiet down.

Then they heard the "Bharatpur Orchestra"—full of chirping and cheeping, cooing and hooting, tweeting and trilling, cawing and warbling! All around them was the music of the birds.

Hardik wrote later, "I would really like to come back here and get used to the singing and beauty of the birds."

"What is a sanctuary?" Sunita asked Ruksana. Ruksana was not quite sure, so Sunita asked Rupa Ma'am.

"A sanctuary is a place where you feel safe," said Rupa Ma'am. "In many places, people have cut down trees and drained wetlands to build houses and factories. These trees and wetlands are the birds' homes and without them birds do not have places where they can live. So a 'bird sanctuary' is a place where many different birds have a safe place to live, with lots of trees and food."

Grey Hornbill

While they were talking, Hardik noticed a bird with a huge beak sitting on a fig tree and eating the fruit. "What kind of food do birds eat?" he asked Doc.

"Birds have very definite food habits," said Doc. "They can generally be divided into those that eat fruit and those that eat fish and worms."

"Eww, worms!" said Punam.

Dilip was a bit upset to hear that birds of prey, like the kestrel, ate other small birds.

Doc told them that every type (species) of bird has its own special food and its own way of getting it from its surroundings (habitat). He said that birds could be broadly divided into those which live in the water and those which live on trees.

The wetland has thousands of birds swimming in the water, some feeding on the surface, others diving under for food. Birds living on trees eat fruits, nectar and insects.

Golden orioles and parakeets are fruit-eaters. Mynas and woodpeckers tap on tree trunks to find insects to eat. Flycatchers, drongos and bee-eaters catch insects when they fly from one juicy fruit or flower to another.

To maintain balance, there were a few birds of prey, which depended on a large number of insects and smaller birds. That's why there were so many mynas, sunbirds and warblers. These smaller birds in turn ate plants. That's why the sanctuary was full of trees and plants, said Doc.

This was an example of a food pyramid—the birds of prey were at the top, smaller birds below them and plants and trees below these birds. The food we eat travels from the farm to the *mandi* to the kitchen and finally, to our plates. In Bharatpur, however, whenever you felt hungry, you could just grab your meal from the tree, water or ground!

Near the edge of the road there was a large, one-metre high mound. A mud castle built by children? No!

It was a skyscraper built by tiny termites!

They had excavated the earth to create a large, hollow home underground to bring up their babies. Just like we control the temperature in our homes using air-conditioning or heaters, the termites controlled the temperature of the mound by building walls and passages. The mound remained dry even in monsoon and thousands of termites built, repaired and protected their colony. Each colony had one queen, who laid all the eggs, which the worker ants looked after. Adult termites grow wings and fly off in the monsoon.

Every few metres the children found termite mounds. "How many millions of termites there must be in this sanctuary!" said Doc.

He told them a dramatic story about a termite mound during a shower of rain. Hundreds of termites flew out of their home like dense clouds, their wings glittering in the light. Many hungry birds had gathered around to catch them. Jungle babblers, mynas and drongos caught the termites as they emerged, before they could fly off. A garden lizard sat comfortably on the mound, catching them one by one—*slurp*!— with its long tongue.

Shrike

"What a feast it was!" said Doc.

Birds could be identified by so many things—their shape, colour, pattern of feathers, and their calls. Dr. Yardi had a guide-book— *The Book of Indian Birds* by Salim Ali. The children excitedly tried to remember the birds they had seen and identify them in the book.

A large bird looked around majestically from its high perch.

"He must be the chief of the birds," whispered Punam. "He is wearing a cap."

Dev saw in the guide-book that the cap was actually a "crest"— it was a crested serpent eagle, so named because it eats snakes!

Seeing a flock of parakeets, Leela said, "Only some of them have red rings around their necks. Why?"

She was surprised to be told that among birds, the males were always more brightly coloured than the females. She wrote later in her diary that the male parakeet "was very beautiful, with a red ring around its neck."

A dark shadow suddenly filled the sky. Ruksana looked up and saw a group of huge birds swooping overhead. The children recognised them as hornbills. They were calling to one another in a lively chorus.

"Even if you don't see them, you know they're there, because you can recognise the call, just as you recognise your friends' voices," said Dr. Yardi.

"Are there people who understand the language of birds?" asked Sunita.

Doc explained that birds use different types of calls for keeping contact with their flock or warning them of danger. Birds also have special songs to attract a mate during the breeding season.

Love songs, thought Dilip and chuckled.

Just then, he heard sweet music. It was a magpie robin, swinging on a branch and singing happily!

Bulbul
Nilgai

They were so busy looking at the birds that they had forgotten there were animals in the sanctuary too! Gauransh noticed a large animal, "very heavy like a horse, but very beautiful." It was part of a herd of nilgai (blue bulls) browsing on the shrubs.

The habitat is home to other small creatures too– jungle cats, jackals, civets and mongoose. There was also a large herd of cattle that made dung piles to mark their separate territories. "The cattle do not belong to anyone," said the guide. "They are feral cattle and have become quite wild."

Up ahead, there was monkey drama!

Some tourists who were carrying food in plastic bags were being followed by groups of monkeys. The guide told the tourists to hide the bags because the monkeys might become aggressive if they were not given food.

There was a whoosh of white overhead and Divyansh looked up to see a group of Egyptian vultures serenely gliding by on outstretched wings. He wistfully remembered trying to fly like birds when he was a little boy.

The vultures soared above his head, catching a thermal current (light, warm air moving upwards). Once they were high up they would be able to spot a dead animal to feed on. From that height, Divyansh must look like a tiny ant!

Greylag geese, on the other hand, were fast flyers in a V-formation. If each bird flew alone, it would have to flap its wings very often, but flying in a large group lowered the wind resistance. This made the birds less tired when they flew long distances from one part of the country to another. The children understood— after all, in school it was much easier to do things in groups rather than alone.

"If I can't fly like a bird," decided Divyansh, "maybe I can be a pilot!"

Egyptian Vultures

In the woodland there was a huge, old, hollow tree. Much of the wood inside had been eaten away by small beetles and ants and used by fungi and bacteria to form new soil.

There was a lot that was invisible in these old trees. "Just imagine," said Doc, "how much carbon there is in all these tree trunks. The tree leaves have taken the carbon from the air and saved it in the trunks over many, many years. The trees in our forests are reducing the harmful effects of climate change and global warming."

All the children wanted to take a picture of themselves with the magnificent tree. *Say cheese*!

Painted Stork

The wetland under the trees was like a crowded railway station! The children were by now becoming good at spotting details and identifying the birds. They saw pintail ducks upend themselves to feed on snails and worms in the mud underwater, while shoveler ducks collected food into their wide bills from the surface.

Egret

Grey Heron

Stilt

"So many different kinds of ducks!" said Leela, looking up from the guide-book.

Jacanas and coots were walking on floating lily-pads with their large feet.

Moorhens pulled out strings of algae and happily gobbled them up!

A tall, black-winged stilt walked on its long legs like a model on a catwalk.

A large grey heron and an egret stood still like statues in the tall grass, waiting for a fish or frog to come close, and then—*flash*!—they would catch it.

A stork waded slowly through the deeper water looking for fish and finally caught a slippery meal after several attempts.

A large darter bird sat on a branch. It is also called a snake bird because of its long, S-shaped neck.

This habitat is also used by many species of fish to lay their eggs. Birds that form nesting colonies on trees around the wetland catch the fish to feed their young ones.

Pond Heron

The children and the adults sat down under a shady tree. Doc pointed below the small bridge where they were sitting. They saw water being pumped out and brought into the wetland by a canal.

“This was made by the maharajas of Bharatpur over a hundred years ago,” said Doc.

“Why?” asked Vinita.

“To bring water to the fields,” said Doc. “The canal distributes monsoon water throughout the wetland all year round. The maharajas and their guests used to shoot birds, so they built the water system in such a way that different birds could feed in it, while raised paths (bunds) could be used by people to walk.”

This shallow wetland system also means that the water that flows in from the lake evaporates, leaving saline water behind. The children found this out when they tried to drink water from the local stall but found it too salty!

Thousands of birds are now getting their food due to the water-level management by the Forest Department.

By now, everyone's water bottles were empty as the temperature had begun to rise. The thirsty children were beginning to feel the midday heat.

They were surprised to learn that this heat is what attracted many birds to Bharatpur. Every winter, birds travelled hundreds of miles from colder places and stayed in warm Bharatpur for a while.

Like a Christmas holiday, thought Gauransh.

"These migratory birds have not been coming to Bharatpur for the past few years, though," said Doc. "The reason is not clear, but maybe they are being killed while in flight. The birds in the sanctuary are protected but outside it, people can still hurt them."

"This is another reason why this sanctuary is a safe place," said Dr. Yardi. "People used to hunt and shoot birds here also but Salim Ali asked Prime Minister Jawaharlal Nehru to make this place a sanctuary."

“Nobody shoots birds here anymore, except with cameras!”

Dilip did not say anything but just like Salim Ali, he too made up his mind that when he grew up, he would not let birds die such a sad death.

After the walk through the sanctuary, the children reached the restaurant and sat down in a circle under the trees to eat their lunch. Hungry jungle babblers came hopping up, looking for scraps of food, but cooked food was not healthy for them as it was not their natural diet. A few minutes later, crows and mynas came up as well. It was quite clear that it was time for the birds to do some human-watching!

Everyone was careful not to spill any food, and no plastic or paper was left behind.

They felt very contented as they walked back to the gate. They had met so many creatures and heard so many musical concerts!

For a few hours the children had felt like fearless explorers, travelling through a different world.

Maybe one day they too would have a bird named after them, just like the Himalayan forest thrush is named *Zoothera salimali*, after Salim Ali, the "Birdman of India." Wouldn't that be exciting?

Thrush

Now it is *Your* Turn!

Imagination Takes Flight!

What route would birds take to reach Bharatpur from Siberia?

Many migratory birds travel from cold Siberia to warm Bharatpur in winter. How would you plan a safe trip for these birds? Do you think the birds will be faster than a train?

Describe a food pyramid for other endangered animals.

You have seen how the food pyramid in Bharatpur sustains many types of birds. What kind of food pyramid would be needed for other species, such as the tiger or the rhino? Try and imagine how different sanctuaries across India balance the needs of all the animals and birds which live in them.

If you could create a new bird, what would it look like?

Now that you know the various identifying features of birds, design a new bird! Give it colour and shape and a nice, fantastic beak. Does it eat worms or fruits or pizza? What will its name be? If you said "Hello!" would it say "caw-caw" or "Namaste" or something else?

See if you understand the language of birds.

The cock crows, but the crow caws. Sparrows tweet and owls hoot. Pigeons coo and geese honk. Can you think of other sounds that birds and animals make while talking to each other?

Try and identify the state tree where you live.

All Indian states have a state tree, which is recognised as one of the official symbols of that state. These trees are native to the region, which means they developed there naturally a long time ago. Native trees are well adapted to environmental conditions of their home regions. Are there any native trees where you live? Describe its leaves, flowers and fruits.

How long can you stand on one leg like a heron?

Many birds like herons and flamingos often stand on one leg for long periods of time. Some scientists think they do this to conserve body heat. Maybe these birds are yoga masters! What would you call this *yogasana*?

First published in India in 2018 by

Mapin Publishing Pvt. Ltd
706 Kaivanna, Panchvati, Ellisbridge
Ahmedabad 380006 INDIA
T: +91 79 40 228 228
F: +91 79 40 228 201
E: mapin@mapinpub.com
www.mapinpub.com

International Distribution

Worldwide (except North America and South Asia)
Prestel Publishing Ltd.
14-17 Wells Street
London W1T 3PD
T: +44 (0)20 7323 5004
F: +44 (0)20 7323 0271
E: sales@prestel-uk.co.uk

North America
Antique Collectors' Club
T: +1 800 252 5231
F: +1 413 529 0862
E: sales@accpublishinggroup.com
www.accpublishinggroup.com/us

South Asia
Mapin Publishing Pvt. Ltd

ISBN: 978-93-85360-48-0
Series ISBN: 978-93-85360-47-3

Series Editor: Narayani Gupta
Copyediting: Mithila Rangarajan / Mapin Editorial
Design and Production:
Gopal Limbad, Darshit Mori /
Mapin Design Studio

Printed in India

The creation of this book was supported by Parag, an initiative of TATA Trusts.

parag
AN INITIATIVE OF TATA TRUSTS

Author: **Dr. Erach Bharucha** is a doctor by day and eco-hero by night! He has been working to preserve India's beautiful natural heritage for many decades now. He enjoys taking children to sanctuaries and other such areas to help them learn about nature, not just from books but also through observation and interaction with the environment. While much of India's natural heritage has been destroyed, Dr. Bharucha is optimistic that children today will later in life be able to protect our forests, rivers and animals.

Artist: As children, **Maya Ramaswamy** and her sisters spent all their play-time with creepy crawlies. Their busy father had a deep respect for life, and taught them that wild creatures were also living beings. Maya grew up with a sense of wonder and love for India's wilderness. She has illustrated several books on wildlife and conservation for children, and she hopes that children will make time to observe birds and to admire butterflies.